# The Whole Green World

by **TONY JOHNSTON**

pictures by **ELISA KLEVEN**

Farrar Straus Giroux / New York

Text copyright © 2005 by the Johnston Family Trust
Illustrations copyright © 2005 by Elisa Kleven
All rights reserved
Distributed in Canada by Douglas & McIntyre Publishing Group
Color separations by Embassy Graphics
Printed and bound in the United States of America by Phoenix Color Corporation
Designed by Nancy Goldenberg
First edition, 2005
1 3 5 7 9 10 8 6 4 2

www.fsgkidsbooks.com

Library of Congress Cataloging-in-Publication Data
Johnston, Tony, date.
   The whole green world / Tony Johnston ; pictures by Elisa Kleven.— 1st ed.
      p.   cm.
   Summary: A rhyming story about planting some seeds.
   ISBN-13: 978-0-374-38400-5
   ISBN-10: 0-374-38400-2
   [1. Nature—Fiction.   2. Stories in rhyme.]   I. Kleven, Elisa, ill.   II. Title.

   PZ8.3.J639 Wh 2005
   [E]—dc21
                                                                                    00-063625

*For Matthias Anjoh (grows tall as a tree) Wehrle*

*And in memory of Frederick Law Olmsted*

—T.J.


*For my good friends Susanna, Kathleen, Marissa, and Sue*

—E.K.

I've got a little pair of shoes.

(Comfy, cozy little shoes.)

Got a little pair of shoes

to walk the whole round world.

I've got a little shaggy dog.
(Lively, lovely, waggy dog.)
Got a little shaggy dog
to tag along with me.

I've got a little pokey stick.

(Okeydokey brittle stick.)

Got a little pokey stick

to dig the whole round world.

I've got a little sack of seeds.

(Fat and slick like glassy beads.)

Got a little sack of seeds

to plant the whole round world.

I've got a little water can.

(Skinny, tinny water can.)

Got a little water can

to wet the whole round world.

I've got a big bright ball of sun.

(Hot enough to brown a bun.)

Got a big bright ball of sun

to warm the whole round world.

I've got some birds to follow me.
(Feathered birds that swallow seeds.)
Got some birds to follow me
around the whole round world.

I've got some ladybugs and ants.

(Ants that love to crawl on plants.)

Got some ladybugs and ants

to crawl the whole round world.

I've got myself a little breeze.

(Sneaky breeze that no one sees.)

Huffy-puffy as you please

to blow seeds round the world.

I've got the tallest, sweetest cake.

(Sweet, tall cake my mama baked.)

Got the tallest, sweetest cake

to eat while my seeds sprout.

I've got a little bitty book.

(Crisp and new and pretty book.)

Got a little bitty book

to read to my good seeds.

I've got a silver smile of moon.

(Nice and icy slice of moon.)

Got a silver smile of moon

to smile on my good seeds.

I've got lots of flowers and trees.

(Mumbling loud with bumblebees.)

I've got lots of flowers and trees.

And that is all I need.

I've got a little pair of shoes.

(How I love my little shoes!)

Got a little pair of shoes

to dance the whole green world.